For all lovers of trees – *E.M*

For my mother, father and Duncan,
who taught me to care for trees – *H.E*

Spirit of the Forest copyright © Frances Lincoln Limited 2002
Text copyright © Helen East and Eric Maddern 2002
Illustrations copyright © Alan Marks 2002
The right of Alan Marks to be identified as the illustrator of this work
has been asserted by him in accordance with the Copyright,
Designs and Patents Act, 1988 (United Kingdom).

First published in Great Britain in 2002 by
Frances Lincoln Limited, 4 Torriano Mews
Torriano Avenue, London NW5 2RZ

www.franceslincoln.com

British Library Cataloguing in Publication Data
available on request

ISBN 0-7112-1863-3 hardback

Set in Bembo

Printed in Singapore

1 3 5 7 9 8 6 4 2

SPIRIT OF THE FOREST

TREE TALES FROM AROUND THE WORLD

Helen East ✦ Eric Maddern

Illustrated by Alan Marks

FRANCES LINCOLN

Contents

How Trees Came to Be

NATIVE NEW ZEALAND

In the beginning, Father Sky and Mother Earth were close, close together, clinging to each other tight, tight, tight. So very close, so very tight, that their children, held between them, had no space to live or breathe. Desperately the young ones wriggled, wrestled, pressed and pushed until at last the sky broke loose. Off and away he floated, up and up and up.

Far below and far behind, he saw his wife the earth outstretched, so beautiful, so brown and smooth – and yet so bare, left all alone. The sky looked down, ashamed to leave her there, all naked.

So he made her ornaments, twisted out of light and dust, rolled into trunks and limbs, curled into leaves and lengths. Brown and red, grey and green, some pinkly blossoming, some silver-starred, some blue-black with berries, some golden with fruit. They were exquisite, scattered like jewels across the soft earth.

The sky was glad, proud to look down.

The earth was glad, proud to be crowned.

The ornaments were proud, glad to adorn the ground. They sank their trunks into the earth, and raised their leaves to the sky. And so you see them standing to this day.

And that, they say, is how trees came to be.

The Stolen Spoons

GREECE

Long ago, when the world was fresh and in the making, and trees walked and talked like any other creatures, Zeus, king of the gods, threw a grand party on Mount Olympus. The music was heavenly, the food divine – even the cutlery glittered. Everyone who was anyone was there, and everyone was impressed.

Zeus himself was pleased ... until he checked the crockery the next day, and found that his silver spoons were missing. It was obvious that one of the guests had stolen them. In a towering rage Zeus despatched the royal cupbearer, Ganymede, down to earth to interrogate the suspects.

First Ganymede went to the Oak, who was outraged. "I am the king of the trees!" he boomed. "I have no need to steal. Besides, I have countless spoon-sized cups, individually tailored to fit each acorn. Why should I want more?"

The Birch was just as indignant. "I am already swathed in sparkling silver from trunk to tips," she hissed. "I don't need any stupid spoons to make me more beautiful!"

"How dare you even ask!" snapped the Elm. "I am far too upright to stoop to such tricks!"

Apologising profusely, poor Ganymede travelled on from tree to tree. He was just about to give up, when he came to the Poplar. Branches bent down behind its back, it was nodding at the horizon, the picture of innocence.

"I don't suppose you know anything about Zeus' spoons, do you, Poplar?" asked Ganymede hopelessly.

"Zeus?" repeated the Poplar, as if it had never heard of him. "Spoons? What spoons?"

Somehow the Poplar sounded a little too innocent. Ganymede looked at the tree more closely. "Why are you holding your branches like that?" he asked, suspiciously.

"Like what?"

"Like that – down behind you, as if you are holding something under them," said Ganymede. "Lift them up. Let me have a look."

The Poplar shrugged, and lifted the tips of its branches a fraction.

"There, look!" it said. "Nothing! Now leave me in peace."

"Higher," insisted Ganymede. "Lift them right up."

The Poplar had no choice. It lifted up its limbs, stretched them out for a second, then hurriedly let them down. But it wasn't quite quick enough. With a tell-tale chiming, chinking rattle, down tumbled the spoons in a silver stream.

"Oooh!" cried the Poplar, looking rather white. "I can't think how they got there!"

But no one believed it.

So that is why, to this very day, the underside of the Poplar's leaves have stayed white with fright like a startled thief – with just a hint of silver from the stolen spoons. And as a punishment, ever since, it has had to hold its branches up, outstretched, to show there is nothing hidden.

The Knot Hole

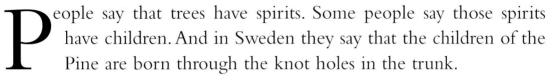

People say that trees have spirits. Some people say those spirits have children. And in Sweden they say that the children of the Pine are born through the knot holes in the trunk.

Now, one day a farmer was walking through the forest, when he heard a baby crying. He hurried towards the sound and found a tiny girl sitting sobbing on a soft pile of pine needles. He looked about and called, but there was no one else around, and as he was a kind-hearted man he didn't want to leave her to the wolves and the bitter blowing wind. So he picked her up, tucked her inside his coat, and took her home to his wife.

The child stayed. She settled in with their own children and soon became as strong and healthy as the rest of them. But as she grew older, although she was the youngest, she grew taller than the tallest, with such a fresh, aloof beauty that it set her quite apart. She was dreamy too; often they'd see her just standing there swaying slightly, eyes closed, singing softly to herself. As if there weren't plenty of things that needed doing! But even her busy mother didn't scold her too much – just gave her a little shake to bring her back to mind. There was something about that girl that was, well, different. It didn't do to waste your breath trying to make her otherwise.

Time passed. The children grew up, and the parents grew old, anxious to see their children settled. Now only the youngest was left, and soon enough a match was arranged for her. He was a fine lad, the son of a neighbouring farmer. She had a good enough dowry, along with her lovely looks. Yes, everyone was happy with the arrangements, and

as soon as they were settled, the young man set to, working long hours to build a new home for his bride.

But as the time approached, the girl seemed more and more withdrawn. Her mother thought nothing of it, but her father began to worry.

The day before the wedding, he found her sitting all alone, sighing, in her room.

"Come, my child," he said, and they wandered out together, arm in arm, across the village and up towards the forest. Right on the edge stood her new home, a lovely little cabin of gleaming, fresh white wood.

"Look at this," said her father. "See how lucky you are? Do not be afraid of leaving your old home."

She stepped inside, breathing deep the cool scent of pine. The walls were rough, hand-hewn, unworn. Her finger followed the grain, still sticky, circling round. One knot hole was not yet blocked. A whisper of wind came through. She bent her eye to the shaft of light, and peeped outside. Endlessly ahead, the woods stood waiting, bowing their heads to her, beckoning her on. The wind was whistling now, a tune that touched her heart. Memories moved her, promises pulled. She tried to turn away, thinking of father, mother, lover – but something stronger stirred. Slowly she slumped, curling like a leaf, shrivelling, squeezing through that tiny space, slipping free to the trees beyond.

By the time her father came in to find his daughter, not a trace remained – only the faintest echo of a tune he thought he knew, a song that came in snatches ever after to comfort him, whenever he walked alone among the deep green pines.

The Yellow-Cedar Sisters

NATIVE NORTH AMERICA

In the beginning, Raven created the world. He brought fresh water to the rivers and put the sun, moon and stars into the sky. He was a clever fellow, but tricky. And he was always hungry – in fact, ravenous.

One day, he was down on the beach when he saw three young women drying salmon. They were graceful girls with long silky hair and smooth skin. But Raven was hungry. He was much more interested in the salmon than the young women. So he came up with a plan to get the fish for himself.

"Aren't you frightened, being here by yourselves?" he asked them.

"No," they said. "We are quite happy to be here alone."

"But are you not afraid of bears?"

"Oh no, we're not scared of bears," they laughed.

"What about wolves?" he asked.

Again they replied, "No."

And so it went on. To every animal Raven named, the women simply shrugged their shoulders and said, "No, we're not afraid of them."

Until he mentioned owls. Suddenly the faces of the young women clouded over.

"Don't talk to us about owls," they said. "We *are* afraid of owls." For the call of owls comes from the spirit world and makes people think of witches and ghosts.

Raven was delighted. At last he could put his plan into action.

He went off into the nearby bushes and began hooting like an owl.

The women didn't realise it was just Raven playing his old tricks. They thought it was a real owl. So they ran off into the forest and kept going until they had climbed halfway up a hill. Then they stopped for breath. They were so tired, they decided to rest for a while.

But as they stood quietly on the mountainside, so frightened they couldn't move up or down, slowly, slowly they began to change. Their still, silent bodies hardened into the trunks of trees. Their feet and toes turned into roots pressing down into the earth. Their arms lifted up to become branches swaying in the breeze. In time, they completely changed into yellow cedar trees. And wily Raven crept back on to the beach and ate all the dried salmon.

And still today, yellow cedars are always found on the high slopes of the western mountain. Still today they are beautiful, their smooth trunks like the skin of a young woman, their silky inner bark like long, shining hair.

The Flame Tree

UGANDA (BUGANDA REGION)

Once there was a man and his wife who had only one child, a daughter. But oh-yeh, what a daughter! Mzuri – beautiful in every way, and growing more so every day. She was sunny-tempered and soft-hearted too. Even the animals, even the birds, even the great sun himself would stop mid-track to look at her. As for the young men, you can imagine, eh?

So of course her parents were happy – everybody was. In those days, such a girl was a blessing for a poor village. She was expected to bring wealth to all when she married.

And so it seemed to be. When she came of age, there was a queue the length and breadth of Buganda. Rich men and strong warriors and great chiefs too, with gifts of cattle and cloth and ornaments of gold and horn and shell. And her father received them all, and wondered which man should be his son-in-law. And her mother fed them all and wondered which man would suit her daughter best.

But the girl? She shook her head. "I want none of them," she said. "For I have already given my heart to Tutu, my childhood friend."

Ai-yai-yai! Tutu was only a poor herdsboy. He had no money to pay for a bride. He stood silently in the shadows outside, while inside everybody cried and shouted and tried to reason with the girl.

Then suddenly – kung! kung! ku-kung! In the middle of all the commotion a messenger arrived from the Sekibobo. The High King was calling his men to war. Mbubi the chief of the Buvuma Islands was advancing across the Blue Lake in a fleet of painted war canoes and every man and youth and boy was needed to beat him back. All the rich men and strong warriors, and great chiefs too, gathered together their followers and set off at once for the great lake. And with them went Tutu the herdsboy, carrying only a stick to fight with.

"Be brave, and win glory," Mzuri told him. "Then perhaps my father will let us marry." But after he had left, she thought again. "Better be safe than hurt," she said to herself. "I shall beg him to stay out of the fiercest fighting."

So she ran after him to the edge of the plain, but the men had gone.

"Quick, Fleet-of-foot!" she called to her friend the antelope, "For you run faster than the fastest man. Hurry to my Tutu, and tell him to come back safely."

The antelope was away at once, but by the time he caught up, the men were already lined up for battle, and Tutu was at the front.

Meanwhile, Mzuri was fierce with anxiety. She climbed up into the hills to watch what was happening. But all she could see was a great cloud of dust as the two armies clashed together.

"Fly, Double-eye!" she called to her friend the hawk, "You who set one eye on the way ahead, the other on the earth below. Hurry to the lake and warn Tutu which way to watch for danger."

The hawk was happy to help, but by the time he reached the lake, the people of Buganda were pushing the islanders back to their canoes, and Tutu was in the midst of the battle in a hail of arrows and stones.

By now, Mzuri was cold with dread. "Chief of the Cloud Land," she called to the sun, "you who shine everywhere, let me ride on your rays! Take me to my Tutu so I can care for him myself!"

The sun stretched down, and catching her up in his bright beams, he swung her high into the air, so that she could see the shore of the lake. The High King had won, and Mbubi's men had fled, but the land was littered with the wounded and the dead. And there amongst the bodies, killed by a stone from an islander's sling, lay Tutu, the brave young herdsman.

"Oh, Chief of the Cloud Land and King of the earth beneath," cried the girl, "let me be with my love at last!"

Then the sun was filled with pity and let her fall to the ground. The High King took pity on her too, and buried her with Tutu, her childhood sweetheart. And out of their grave grew a wonderful tree, with smooth brown bark that the antelopes came to rub against, and graceful outstretched branches where the hawk settled to sleep, and big flame-coloured blossoms reaching up to draw the sun. It was so beautiful that everyone liked to look at it. Lovers walked under it, children played round it, and its seeds were taken far and wide to plant in gardens everywhere.

So it spread, and now it blesses even the poorest villages with its beauty. People throughout the world call it the Flame Tree. But in Buganda, the old people remember this story and they call the tree Kifabakazi, for they know that inside, it is as soft as a lover's heart.

The Green Ladies
of One Tree Hill

ENGLAND

Once there was a farmer who had three sons. Though his land was poor, his cows gave the sweetest milk, his sheep the finest wool, and his hens the finest eggs. The reason for his good fortune was this: on top of a hill near the edge of his land grew three beautiful beech trees. Every Midsummer Eve he would make three posies of late primroses and place them in the roots of these trees. And on nights when the moon was full, strange fairy music played and around the shining beech trees three Green Ladies danced.

When the farmer grew old, he called his three sons to him and said, "Our luck here depends on that hill. Don't forget to do what I have always done, like my father before me and his father and grandfather before him. Honour the three Green Ladies of that hill, and all will be well." Not long afterwards, the old man died.

When the land was divided up, the biggest slice went to the oldest brother. The next brother took the best of the rest, leaving the youngest only a poor strip of ground at the foot of the hill. With it went a broken-down cottage, one skinny cow, a couple of moth-eaten sheep and a few scrawny chickens. But the lad didn't complain. He set about his work with a whistle and a song, and when next Midsummer came, he remembered his father's advice. He took posies of fresh primroses up the hill and laid them in the roots of the three beech trees. And on moonlit nights, wild haunting music played and the three Green Ladies danced.

The youngest brother did well. The barley heads swelled in his lit-tle field; his trees were loaded with fruit. His herbs grew sweet and green, and his cow gave the creamiest milk.

As for the other two brothers, they didn't bother putting posies on the hill. Maybe they forgot. Maybe they were lazy. Maybe they just didn't believe that oldfashioned nonsense any more. But their farms did not do well. Their crops wilted, their cows grew thin, their hens all ran away. When they saw how successful their youngest brother was, jealousy began to eat them inside until it burst out in a boiling rage.

The oldest brother went to the youngest and said, "I see you're doing well, and I've seen you on top of that hill."

"Yes," replied the youngest brother, "I work hard – and I do go up there from time to time."

"Well, you'll not be going up there any more!" shouted the oldest brother. "That is my land and if you go up there, you're trespassing. What's more," he added, "tomorrow I'm going to cut those three trees down and use them for building my barn."

The oldest brother was true to his word. Next morning he was at the foot of the hill with horses and carts and men with sharpened axes. But when the men saw what he wanted them to do, they refused. "We can't do that," they said. "We've seen the Green Ladies dance. We don't know what will happen if we cut down those trees."

In a fury, the oldest brother snatched up an axe, strode up the hill and brought it swinging down through the air... CHOP! into the side of the tree. It screamed like a woman in pain. But he paid no heed. As he chopped and chopped, wood chips flew and the screams became weaker, until the tree began to fall. But somehow it twisted and crashed on to the older brother, killing him stone dead.

The workmen took away the body of the man and the body of the tree, and from that day on, only two Green Ladies danced on moonlit nights.

The middle brother took both farms for himself, while the youngest still worked his strip and took primroses up the hill on Midsummer Eve. And while the youngest brother did well, the middle brother did badly. At last he could bear it no longer.

In a rage, he went to the youngest brother and said, "Why are you doing so well? What are you doing on that hill?"

The youngest brother replied quietly, "I am lucky, and I go up on the hill when I feel the need."

"Well, that's my land and you'll not go up there any more!" bellowed the middle brother. "Besides," he added, "tomorrow I'm going to cut those two trees down."

He must have completely forgotten what had happened to his brother.

Once again the workmen refused to help. Once again, the brother took up an axe, climbed up the hill and began chopping a tree. Once again the air was filled with a woman's screams. This time the tree fell cleanly to the ground. The middle brother leaned on his axe and smiled triumphantly at the men below.

But suddenly there was a loud crack, and a single branch fell from the last tree, knocking the brother on the head. When the men went up, they found him lying dead over the tree he had just cut down..

They took away the body of the man and the body of the tree and, when the burying was done, the youngest brother inherited all three farms. But he still lived in his little cottage near the hill, now with just the one Green Lady. And every Midsummer Eve he still took three primrose posies up the hill, one for the tall, beautiful beech; the others he laid upon the two stumps. And on moonlit nights, if you were lucky, you could just see one Green Lady dancing to the faintest fairy music. And his farm continued to thrive.

Today that hill is covered with beech trees. I don't know if anyone takes primrose posies up there now on Midsummer's Eve, but if not, maybe someone should.

Rhododendron and Little Alder

NEPAL

High, high, mountain meets sky. Life is scratched from thin earth, snatched from thin air. Only the Rhododendron blooms proudly, all alone.

But once upon a time, they say, Rhododendron longed for company. Wrapped in the winds of winter he looked down, far below, to where the little Alder tree struggled on the slopes.

"Gentle Alder Tree," he roared, "I am your overlord. Yet I wish to honour you, humble as you are. You and I can intertwine; I will help you in your climb. Only say that you'll be mine, and my heights will be yours."

Alder stared. She saw only a plain bush bare of bloom, its leaves curled from cold.

Proudly she tossed her branches, turned away from his advances. "My sap runs royal red. You're no match for me!" she said.

But when the warmth of summer came, Rhododendron up above blossomed crimson, purple, white. Dazzled by the gorgeous sight, Little Alder fell in love with him. Now she did her best to please, shimmering her bark and leaves, but her efforts were in vain. Rhododendron, still offended, would not even glance at her.

At last Alder, broken-hearted, tore up her roots and flung herself down the mountainside. As she fell, her flailing branches dragged down rocks and set off avalanches.

So, to this day, when there is a big rockfall, Nepali people say it is Little Alder's fault. And if you look, you'll always find her in amongst the débris, clinging to the rocks, while high above, Rhododendron looks the other way.

The Tree with Three Fruits

WALES

Long ago in Wales, there lived a wise old saint called Illtud. One day the old man was sitting by his fire when he nodded off and the fire went out. Illtud had a young disciple called Baglan, who saw what had happened and decided to help. He went to his own fire, knelt down, and scraped some hot coals into his cloak. Then he carried them over and tipped them into Illtud's fireplace.

Suddenly the old man woke up and saw that Baglan had carried the coals in his cloak. But there were no holes, no burn marks. It was a miracle! Illtud thought to himself, "Baglan must be a truly holy man."

Next day, Illtud called Baglan and said, "Take this brass-handled crook and walk over the hills and dales of Wales until you find a tree with three fruits. There I want you to build a church."

So Baglan set out, walking across the land with his brass-handled crook, looking everywhere for a tree with three fruits. Would it be apples, mulberries and pears? Or hazelnuts, cherries and plums? He didn't know. He wanted to find this marvellous tree. But though the brass-handled crook seemed to guide him on his way, he found nothing.

At last he sat down to rest beneath the spreading branches of a mighty oak tree. He was just dozing off when he heard grunting. A sow with her litter of piglets was rooting about in the acorns. Baglan smiled.

Then he noticed halfway up the tree a hole with wild bees flying in and out. Mmmm, he thought, honey. At that moment a bird began to warble a beautiful tune high in the tree. He leapt to his feet, looked up and saw a nest of blackbirds.

Suddenly it hit him: these were the three fruits! Piglets, honey, and birdsong!

Baglan laughed out loud. So it was here he had to build a church. But the ground was rocky and rough around the tree, not a good place for a building. Nearby was a flat meadow, so Baglan decided to build there. He began digging the foundations and carrying big stones for the wall. Soon the walls were knee-high.

That night, he slept soundly in his bracken bed. But next morning, when he came back, there was water in the foundations and the stone walls had tumbled down!

"How strange," thought Baglan. Still, he wasn't one to give up easily. So he carried on, working harder than before. By evening, the walls were waist-high. That night he slept even more soundly, but in the morning, once again, there was water in the foundations and the stone walls had tumbled down.

"Very peculiar," said Baglan. But he was a stubborn man and determined to succeed. So he worked harder than ever, and at the day's end the walls of his little church were chest-high. He went to his bracken bed and slept better than ever before. But in the morning, when he came back ... water in the foundations, stone walls tumbled down.

This time he thought, "Maybe someone's trying to tell me something. Perhaps this is the wrong place for the church." So he went back to the old oak, the tree with the three fruits, looked at it and thought, "Maybe I could build a church around the tree".

And that is what he did. The animals helped him. The pigs dug the foundations with their snouts, the birds brought crusts of bread and the bees supplied him with honey. When it was finished it was rather higgledy-piggledy, but it was still a beautiful little church. He made sure there was a door at the bottom for the old mother sow, a hatch halfway up for the bees, and in the topmost branches, a skylight for the birds.

When he had finished, Baglan sat outside scratching the back of the old sow with his brass-handled crook. The blackbirds roosted on his shoulders, the bees flew about his head like a halo. People came from miles around to see Baglan and his wonderful church. And they loved to see the way he had with animals and birds of the forest ... a Welsh St Francis.

But finally the time came, as it comes to us all, when Baglan had to leave this Earth. And now there's nothing left but a pile of stones and this story – the story of Baglan and the Tree with Three Fruits.

The Coconut Fisherman

New Guinea

Well, you know how it is: some people are always going to go their own way. They always did, and they always will. So when, at the very beginning of time, the people of New Ireland agreed it would be best if everyone did everything – a bit of fishing, a bit of farming, a bit of hunting – one man did not fall in line with everyone else.

"I am a fisherman," he said. "That's what I know, that's what I do. I'm not going to spend my time poking around waiting for things to come out of the dull brown earth, when I could be out on the bright blue sea, gathering the food that is waiting for me."

"But it is fairer to share," the others explained. "We should all take our turn at everything."

"Not me," said the fisherman, and away he went about his own business.

Now maybe he was the best at catching fish, and perhaps others were better than him at making gardens and growing vegetables. But that wasn't the point. The villagers were annoyed, and decided to teach him a lesson.

"Let him look to himself, then," they cried, "and keep his fish too. Why should we want fish rather than the yams and taro that we have worked so hard to grow, or the sweetness of honey found deep in the forest?"

And so, when the fisherman returned with his catch that night, he found himself cut off from the rest of the village. No one would speak to him, no one would even greet him, and certainly no one would eat with him, or barter one dish for another.

Tired though he was after a long day out on the water, the poor man struggled on from door to door, until he came to the edge of the forest. By now it was quite dark.

"Perhaps I could find a wild yam or two," he said sadly, making himself a split bamboo torch to light the way. Deep among the trees, he came at last to a likely place and tied the torch on to his back, so he could see where he was digging.

But as he bent low to reach for a root, the flame suddenly spurted, setting fire to his hair. Down he fell headlong, with no one to help, and died in the hole he had dug for himself.

When they found him next day, the villagers were sorry for their behaviour. But they said, as they buried him where he lay, "This was a man who chose his own way."

And perhaps he might have been forgotten, had it not been for a strange little shoot that grew up from his grave. By and by it thickened from a stem to a trunk, and after many months it put out long leaves. No one knew what it could be, but everyone helped take care of it.

A year, later the tree grew round green fruit, and every day the village children came to see if the fruit had ripened. When at last one dropped to the ground, the whole island gathered to see what was inside.

Inside a thick green husk they found a nut the size of a man's head. It was rough and brown as a weatherbeaten face, with two eye-holes and a mouth below.

Then the islanders understood. The fisherman had returned! But this time, instead of fish, he had brought them food and drink: sweet coconut water inside creamy soft flesh that hardened into fine white nut.

And so it was that the man who had never grown crops in his life, through his death brought the finest one of all.

The Willow Tree

JAPAN

Long ago, in a small village near Kyoto, there lived a young farmer called Heitaro.

Every day he worked from dawn to dusk, bent double in the fields. Every evening, just as his father had done before him, he sat talking with his neighbours from dusk until dark, beneath the village willow tree. This was how things had always been, and, people supposed, how things would always be ...

But one day, messengers arrived from the Emperor. They were looking for wood to build a great temple in the city, in honour of Kwannon, the Goddess of Mercy. They wanted the willow tree.

The villagers were sad, but they wanted to give their best to Kwannon. The only one to object was Heitaro.

"This tree is the heart of our village!" he cried. "We cannot let it go. I have several smaller trees by my house. Let the Emperor take those instead." So it was agreed, and the very next day all Heitaro's trees were cut down and carried away.

That night, the moon seemed strangely bright. With no trees left to shield him from its light, Heitaro could not sleep. He got up and went out for a walk, heading for comfort towards the great willow tree.

To his surprise, a stranger stood there, half-hidden in the shadows, her face a fragile flower petal peeping out at him. She was so beautiful, he could only stare, then stammer as she slipped away, "No! Don't go ..."

"I must," she whispered.

"Then come back again. Tomorrow, as the sun sets I'll wait for you here."

Did she say yes? Or was it just the breeze?

From that moment on, Heitaro could think of nothing but her. Next day he worked like a madman, afraid to hope. In the evening, meeting friends beneath the willow, he hardly heard a word they said, only wanting them to go. Then waiting, waiting, waiting, all alone ...

And then she came ... and stayed ... and talked, though she would not tell her name. But she smiled when he told her he would call her Higo, which means Little Willow Friend. And, better still, she promised him that she would return again.

Night by night and week by week they met, and talked, and fell in love. At last she gave in to his pleading, and Heitaro brought his Higo home to marry him. The whole village turned out to welcome her, and danced at their wedding until their feet were sore. And when, a year later, they were blessed with a son, happy Heitaro was the envy of everyone. So the years passed, and so, people supposed, things would always be ...

But one day, messengers arrived from the Emperor. They needed more wood to build Kwannon's great temple in the city. They wanted to take the village willow tree.

Everyone was sad, including Heitaro, but now he had no other trees to offer and there was nothing he could do. Besides, although he still liked to sit with his friends under the tree, he never lingered – his heart was at home with his family. All the same, the next day, when the Emperor's men were cutting down the old willow, he stayed out longer than usual, for he did not want to see it done. And then he took the long way home, to avoid the middle of the village.

By the time he reached home it was getting dark. To his surprise, there were no lights burning, nor the smell of supper cooking. Suddenly afraid, he hurried inside. His little son sat sobbing on the ground.

"Where is your mother?" Heitaro asked, but in his heart he already knew.

"With each cut," said the child, "each blow that struck the willow, my mother moaned, as if she herself were hurt. As it shuddered and juddered, she began to tremble. When it fell with a groan, she fell too. But as she touched the ground, she vanished into mist with a sigh and a cry, and a last loving kiss."

Gathering the boy up into his arms, Heitaro went sorrowfully into the village. The old willow lay stretched out like a corpse across the ground, sap still dribbling from its torn trunk. The leaves quivered as they approached. Was it the breeze, or Higo whispering goodbye?

One branch had been broken as it fell; unwanted, it was tossed aside. Heavy though it was, Heitaro and his son carried it home – but in the half-light, it seemed almost as if the branch was carrying the child.

They say that Heitaro carved a bed for the boy from the willow-tree wood that linked him with his Higo. And when his son lay down to sleep, he was soothed by the sound of his mother singing.

They say the boy became a great artist, who could paint trees you'd swear lived and breathed. And they say, too, that when he was old, he always smoked a willow-wood pipe, and the smoke that wreathed around his head would take the shape of a beautiful woman. When no one was watching, he'd talk to her, just as if he was talking to his own flesh and blood ...

Kooboo and the Gum Tree

NATIVE AUSTRALIA

The eucalyptus, or gum tree as it's also known, has smooth grey bark and brown peeling patches, silver-green leaf tongues that rattle in the breeze. It grows by the creek beds and in the wide open bushlands of an ancient country far to the south.

And up in some eucalyptus – river-red-and-blue gums, manna, swamp and forest gums – high in their branches, sleeping in the sunshine is Kooboo the Koala. He wakes late in the afternoon, climbs a little higher, reaches, picks and munches on a fistful of leaves. Sometimes he comes down, scampers across the leafy ground and scuttles up another tree, safe on high.

Mostly he just sits there chewing eucalyptus leaves, and he never even takes a drink to keep from getting dry. So how does he get by? If you really want to know, this is his story.

Kooboo was an orphan boy with no one to care for him. His relatives didn't even give him any food, so the poor lad had nothing to eat but leaves, the tough, strong-smelling leaves of the eucalyptus trees. Worse than this was his thirst. He lived in a dry place. The people kept their precious water in bark buckets and would only allow him to drink one mouthful a day. He was always begging for water. But somehow he managed to keep himself alive.

At the driest time of the year, the people hid their water buckets when they went hunting. But one day, when Kooboo was wandering around crying from thirst and loneliness, he stumbled on the water buckets hidden in the hollows of a gum tree.

"What luck," the little boy said to himself, and he plunged his head into a bucket and drank and drank until he could drink no more. "How wonderful! At last I have quenched my thirst."

Then he began plotting a way to keep the water for himself. He took the buckets one by one and hung them in the branches of a young gum sapling. Then he climbed up, settled into a fork and began to chant a magical song.

The tree must have felt sympathy for Kooboo, for it grew and grew, carrying him and the water buckets high into the air until it was the tallest tree in the forest. He smiled and thought, "Now I shall never be thirsty again."

That evening, when the people returned from their hunting, they were tired and thirsty. When they couldn't find their water buckets, they were furious. As they were looking for the thief's tracks in the sand, a sharp-eyed woman spotted Kooboo sitting high in the upper branches of a tall eucalyptus tree, surrounded by the water buckets.

"Bring down those water buckets at once, or you'll be in trouble!" called out the men. But Kooboo felt safe in his high place and just laughed. "You hardly gave me any water before," he cried out cheekily. "Now you can get your own water."

At first, no one would dare climb such a high tree. But when the children began crying with thirst, the old men persuaded some youths to try. From up high, Kooboo watched two young men begin their climb. When they were halfway up, he broke off an old branch and dropped it on their heads. They lost their grip and fell to the ground.

This happened several times, until two young medicine men worked out a clever plan. They climbed round and round the trunk of the tree in a spiral, so when Kooboo dropped branches on their heads, he missed, for they had already moved on to another place. As they came closer to Kooboo, he began crying out with fear and begged for mercy. But the young medicine men showed him no mercy. They pulled Kooboo from his seat in the tree and threw him down to the ground.

But at that moment the tree must have given Kooboo magical protection. For as soon as his body hit the ground, he turned into a little koala bear and quickly scampered up another tall tree.

So Kooboo, once the little orphan boy, now lives in the eucalyptus tree. He sleeps all day and at night climbs about, munching on the gum leaves. The tree still cares for him, giving him magical protection and providing him with everything he needs. He has a safe home, he is happy eating gum leaves, and he never has to come down from the tree to drink. Maybe he still has those water buckets hidden in the hollows of the eucalyptus trees. Or maybe he gets the water he needs from the leaves. Either way, his name "koala" means "The One Who Never Drinks Water"!

The Silver Birch

GERMAN

A poor girl, a shepherdess, was walking through the wood searching for a lost sheep, fingers busy as she went, spinning little bits of wool found tangled in the bushes. But oh! she was tired. She sat down for a rest, leaning her back against a white birch trunk.

Then she thought she was dreaming, for suddenly the tree began to curve and sway against her, and looking up into its branches, she imagined she saw a face looking down at her – a lovely face, a wooden one, with bark for skin, yet like a lady too, and it seemed to be leaning down and smiling at her.

Was she scared? Of course! She jumped up to run, but the birch face called down to her, soft as the rustling of leaves.

"Child, stay! Don't run away. Stop a while and let me look at you, at your little white feet, each step so sweet. Imagine what it's like for me. I'm rooted deep into the ground. I cannot dance or walk around. Dance for me, child, just for a while …"

What would *you* do? The girl was afraid, yes, but she was sorry for the tree too. What harm was there in dancing a little?

She skipped and tripped, lightly, brightly, once round the tree, and as she passed a low-hanging branch, caught hold of it as if it were an arm outstretched to swing her. And the branch held fast to her, like a hand gripping her tight, and the tree began to quicken, and its roots trembled and shook deep-down-below-down, until all of a sudden the tree heaved itself up – and out of the earth altogether.

Now they were dancing, both of them together, faster and faster, wilder and wilder. The girl ran out of breath and she wanted to stop, but the tree would not.

The day went past and still they danced. Dusk fell, yet they went on.

Then the shepherdess began to cry, "Please, birch tree! My feet are so sore. Please let me rest. I can't dance any more!"

Just as she neared despair, sure that the birch tree didn't care, it tossed her in the air, caught and cradled her like a baby, its branch brushing a cat's-kiss touch, then softly laid her down. And the birch tree sighed, as it sank back down and settled in the ground.

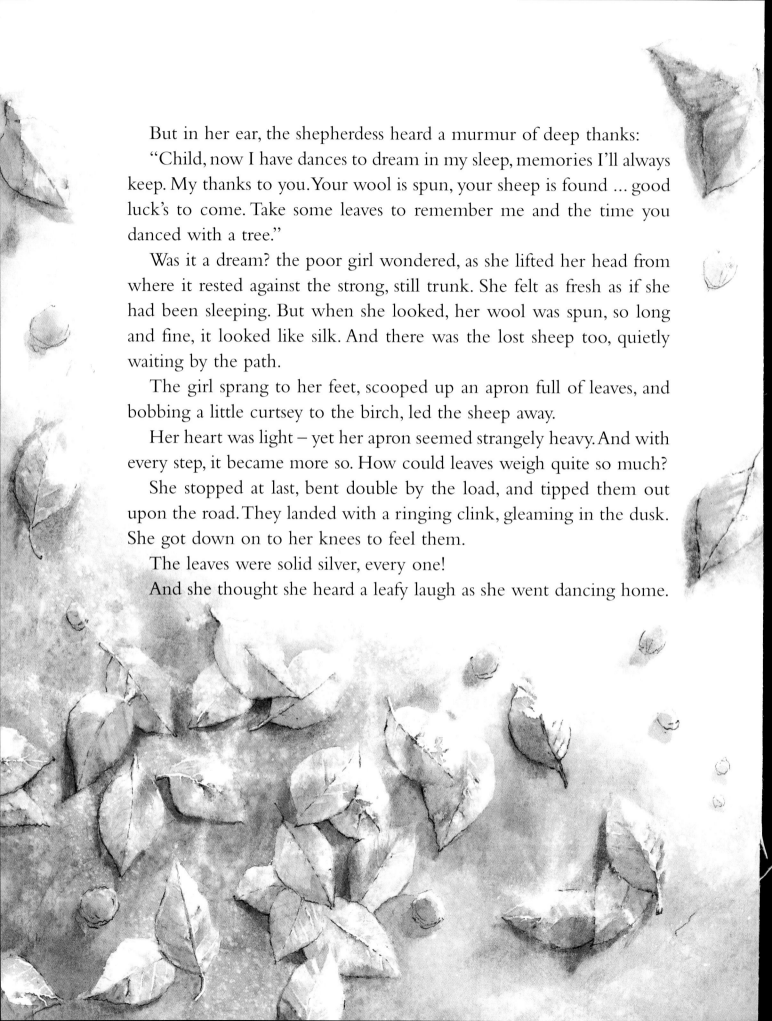

But in her ear, the shepherdess heard a murmur of deep thanks:

"Child, now I have dances to dream in my sleep, memories I'll always keep. My thanks to you. Your wool is spun, your sheep is found … good luck's to come. Take some leaves to remember me and the time you danced with a tree."

Was it a dream? the poor girl wondered, as she lifted her head from where it rested against the strong, still trunk. She felt as fresh as if she had been sleeping. But when she looked, her wool was spun, so long and fine, it looked like silk. And there was the lost sheep too, quietly waiting by the path.

The girl sprang to her feet, scooped up an apron full of leaves, and bobbing a little curtsey to the birch, led the sheep away.

Her heart was light – yet her apron seemed strangely heavy. And with every step, it became more so. How could leaves weigh quite so much?

She stopped at last, bent double by the load, and tipped them out upon the road. They landed with a ringing clink, gleaming in the dusk. She got down on to her knees to feel them.

The leaves were solid silver, every one!

And she thought she heard a leafy laugh as she went dancing home.

About the Stories

How Trees Came to Be - *Indigenous New Zealand*
In some versions of this myth, the Sky places the trees upside-down, but then decides they don't look right.

The Stolen Spoons - *Ancient Greece*
Told to me by a teacher in Gossops Green, who heard it from her father; also referred to in C.M.Skinner's *Myths and Legends of Flowers, Trees, Fruits and Plants* by J.B. Lippincott, (Philadelphia/London, 1925). The poplar is generally considered untrustworthy and a gossip because its leaves tremble so.

The Knot Hole - *Sweden*
Various versions exist in Norway and Sweden. This one, from Småland, is referred to in C.M.Skinner's *Myths and Legends of Flowers, Trees, Fruits and Plants*. The pine tree is associated with goodness in Europe and Asia, but in native American folklore it is often portrayed as selfish and inflexible.

The Yellow-Cedar Sisters - *Indigenous North America*
Originally told by Alice Paul and included in *Ethnobotany of the Hesquiat Indians of Vancouver*, by Nancy J. Turner and Barbara S. Efrat (Westcoast). Adapted from a version told in *Cedar* by Hilary Stewart.

The Flame Tree - *Uganda*
Retold from Mrs George Baskerville's *The Flame Tree and Other Ugandan Folklore Tales* (The Sheldon Press, 1920). The name *Kifabakazi* means "one with a soft spot for women".

The Green Ladies of One Tree Hill - *England and Ireland*
An old English folktale found in Somerset and Derbyshire, first recorded in *Forgotten Tales of the English Counties* by Ruth Tongue (Routledge & Kegan Paul,1970). Also found in *The Wildwood King* by Phillip Kane (Capell Bann, 1997). Even today in West Africa, trees are often seen, in some circumstances, as dancing women. Primroses in May and June were regarded as specially magical plants.

Rhododendron and Little Alder - *Nepal*
Told to Tricia East by her Nepali colleague, Udhap Khaddke (thanks to Eco Himal Non-Government Organisation, Salzburg/Kathmandu). Rhododendrons, which are poisonous, are used to treat snake-bite. The rhododendron flower is the national symbol of Nepal.

The Tree with Three Fruits - *Wales and England*
A traditional Welsh saint's story dating from the 6th century AD. Illtud founded the first monastic college in Britain and is said to have taught St Patrick and St David. This version derives from *Welsh Legends and Folk Tales* by Gwyn Jones. The stone remains of the original small church can still be seen.

The Coconut Fisherman - *Papua New Guinea*
Found in Ulli Beier's collection *When the Moon was Big* (William Collins, Australia, 1972). and first told by the storyteller Gad Mitir. Coconuts are a source of life: in the Pacific they are planted to commemorate a birth, while in India they are used in Hindu marriage ceremonies.

The Weeping Willow - *Japan*
Known throughout Japan. I first heard this from the storyteller Beulah Candappa. I have added the final details from a Czech version of the story. In western Europe the willow tree is usually portrayed as unfriendly.

Kooboo and the Gum Tree - *Australia*
Recorded by Charles Mountford and first written down in *The Dreamtime: Australian Aboriginal Myths* (Rigby, 1965). In 1976 he published a different version in *Before Time Began* (Nelson)

The Silver Birch - *Germany*
Told in Grohmann's *Aberglauben aus Bohmen* and retold in Angel de Gubernatis' *La Mythologie des Plantes* (C.Reinwald et Cie, 1878). In Russia the birch represents health, while in England it is traditionally associated with witches.

Thanks also to: Pliny (Natural History); Kew Gardens; the Scottish Forestry Commission; Ian Darwin Edwards; the Botanical Gardens, Edinburgh; Kavi and Leela Mahipat, Malcolm Green, Duncan Williamson and the many other storytellers who told us tree tales.